Spiros
Soup-Eating
Dinosaur

By Mary E. Ciesa

ISBN 978-0578-879390

Dedicated to my mother, Artemis Nurches;
to Dr. Harry N. Papas, from the Greek "onion
village" of Paleomonastiro; and to my Pappou,
Spiros Nurches. — Mary

Dedicated to Dr. Nate Bergman, thank you;
and to my grandparents who taught me how to
make delicious Avgolemeno soup. — Kristina

It started with one big, blubbery "AHH-CHH-OOO!"
The sneeze was so loud it shook the church bell and
startled the villagers out of their beds.

It was so loud it shook the lemons
on the trees and the onions
out of the ground.

"Here comes our dinosaur Spiros," said little Popi.

Popi plugged her ears. "Poor Spiros! Good thing I know what to give him when he's sick."

Mrs. Koula, the village nurse, couldn't remember what to do. "Hmm, he doesn't eat just vegetables, so he's not a *herbivore*. And he doesn't eat just meat, so he's not a *carnivore*."

Popi interrupted. "Our village dinosaur is an *Avgolemonore* -- because he eats avgolemono soup!"

"Ah yes!" said Mrs. Koula. "It will help him get better. If not, his coughs and sneezes will launch the onions out of the ground and into the air! Then what will we have to sell at the market? What can we do?"

Popi blurted out, "I can help! I remember the soup song you taught me!"

Eggs and lemon,
Chicken and rice,
Onions for flavor,
Yum, it's so nice!

Mrs. Koula lit a cooking fire and poured chicken broth into a large pot. The pot began to tremble, and the broth sloshed from side to side.
"AHH-CHH-OOO!"

"Spiros feels awful!" cried Popi.

"No worries," said Mrs. Koula. "Popi, please sing the soup song again."

Eggs and lemon,
Chicken and rice,
Onions for flavor,
Yum, it's so nice!

"Yes, that's it!" replied Mrs. Koula. "Eggs from the hens!" Popi went to the chicken coop and helped Mrs. Koula gather eggs.

Mrs. Koula shouted, "Lemons from our lemon tree!"
Popi plucked lemons from the lemon tree, and they fell,
ker-plunk! Mrs. Koula carried them in her apron.

"Rice!" reminded Popi.
Mrs. Koula picked up a sack of rice and balanced it on her head.

"Onions for flavor!" said Mrs. Koula.
Popi pulled onions from the field and stuffed them into her apron pockets.

They scurried back to the village square.

On a large, round wooden board, they chopped, chopped, chopped the onions.

"Mmm," inhaled Mrs. Koula. "Our onions smell so delicious. No wonder everyone wants to buy them!"

She put them in the pot of boiling broth, and Popi stirred it once, twice, added the rice, and stirred it thrice. Then she covered it with a heavy lid.

"KAA-KAA-POUIE!" slobbered Spiros.

"Quick!" said Mrs. Koula. Popi beat the egg whites until they were stiff and added lemon juice.

Mrs. Koula slowly poured the eggs into the broth while Popi stirred it with a big wooden spoon. The aroma drifted on the wind to the feverish dinosaur.

"Spiros really needs soup!" urged Mrs. Koula.
Popi called out,

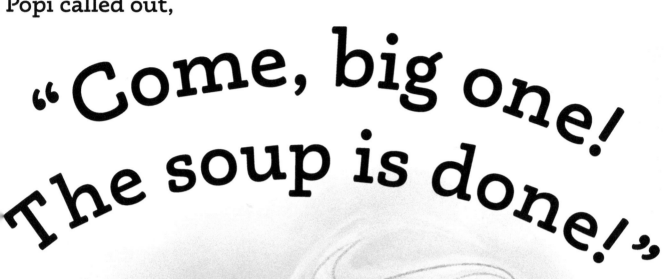

"Come, big one! The soup is done!"

Eggs and lemon,
Chicken and rice,
Onions for flavor,
Yum, it's so nice!

Spiros lumbered into town,

slurped down the soup,

and felt his nose unplug.

He grinned like a baby, then fell asleep in the village square. His fat belly rose and fell with every snore. Instead o a grumble, or a roar, or an "AHH-CHH-OOO," people heard,

"Hee-bee-bee, Hee-bee-bee."

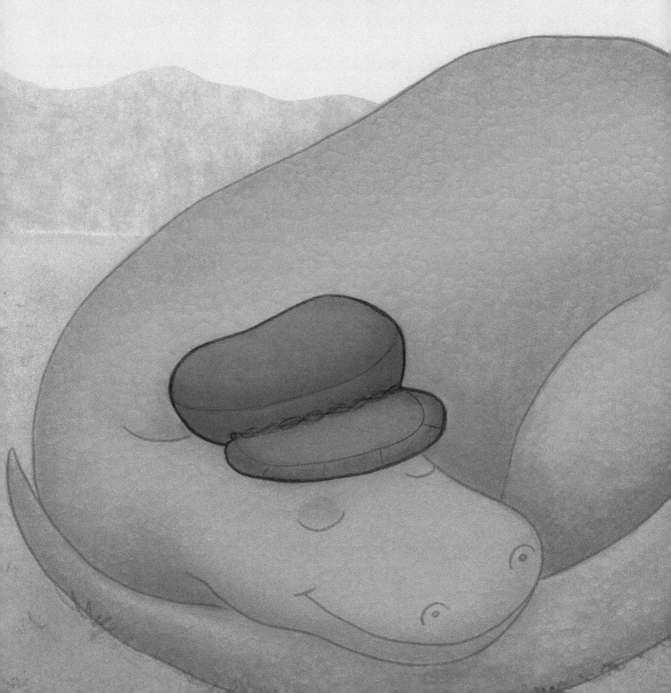

Popi said, "Thank goodness the soup is helping Spiros our dinosaur get better. Now our onions won't be ruined by a blasting dinosaur sneeze."

"And we can still sell them at the market!" said Mrs. Koula.

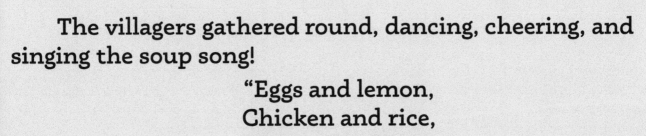

The villagers gathered round, dancing, cheering, and singing the soup song!

"Eggs and lemon,
Chicken and rice,
Onions for flavor,
Yum, it's so nice!"

AVGOLEMONO SOUP RECIPE

Avgolemono (ahv-goh-LEH-moh-noh) soup is a traditional Greek soup. In the Greek language, "avgo" means egg, and "lemono" means lemon. The recipe has been passed down from memory for generations in my family for as long as anyone can remember. It is a well-known Sunday meal, as well as a remedy for the common cold.

8 cups prepared chicken broth (Or make your own. See recipe below)*
1 large onion, chopped
Salt to taste
1 cup white rice
3 eggs, separated
Juice of 1 lemon

In a large pot, add chopped onion to the chicken broth, bring to a boil, cover, reduce heat, and simmer for 1 hour. Strain broth into a clean pot.

** Return broth to a rolling boil. Stir once, twice, add the rice, and stir it thrice. Cover with a heavy lid. After about 15 minutes, lower the heat and let it simmer until the rice is tender. Salt to taste.

Meanwhile, in a large mixing bowl, beat 3 egg whites until stiff, using a hand mixer or electric mixer. Whisk the egg yolks and fold them into the whites. Add the juice of 1 lemon slowly, beating well. (More lemons make it more lemony.) Take a ladleful of soup broth and add it to the egg mixture in a slow, steady stream, whisking all the while. Repeat with a second ladleful. Then pour this mixture back into the pot, stirring well so it doesn't curdle. Heat through, but do not let it boil. Serve and enjoy!

* To make your own chicken broth:

1 4-pound chicken (or 3 pounds of chicken necks, backs, and wings)
1-2 quarts of water
1 onion, chopped
1 teaspoon salt

In a large pot, cover chicken with water. Bring to a boil. Skim off any froth that floats to the top. Add chopped onion and salt. Reduce heat, cover and simmer for 2 hours. Strain broth into a clean pot and continue the soup recipe above at **.

Set cooked chicken aside. (It can be chopped into bite-sized pieces. Add as